WONDER WOMEN

FROM THE HOLY BIBLE

MARIA ISKANDER

Wonder Women
From the Holy Bible
Copyright © MARIA ISKANDER
First published 2024

Published with the assistance of Angel Key Publications
https://angelkey.com.au

Contents

Dedication

I would like to dedicate this book, first and foremost, to Suzan Iskander.

Thank you for being my marvellous mother. You are the epitome of a Wonder Woman.

You have read all my books and writings since I was a child. I am so grateful for your support. I am also proud to have you in my life.

My love for you is eternal.

Disclaimer:

This book is NO substitute for the Holy Bible's recount of the impactful women examined. Each woman examined, has an image of them, followed by a personalied short passage.

Biblical women OMITTED in this book due to limited and/or conflicting information (alphabetical order):

Abihail. Abishag. Abital. Achsah. Adah. Ahinoam. Aholibamah. Asenath. Ashtoreth. Atarah. Atahliah. Azuba. Baara. Basemath. Berenice. Bilhah. Bithiah. Cozbi. Damaris. Delilah. Drusilla. Eglah. Ephah. Ephrath. Hagar. Herodia. Haggith. Hammolekheth. Hamutal. Hazzelelponi. Helah. Hephziba. Hodesh. Hogla. Huldah. Hushim. Iscah. Jecholiah. Jedidah. Jehoaddan. Jerioth. Jerusha. Jezebel. Keturah. Lo-Ruhamah. Maacah I, Maacah II. Mahalath. Mahlah. Matred. Mehetabel. Me-Zahab. Mother of King Lemuel. Naamah. Naarah. Noa. Noadiah. Peninnah. Persis. Puah. Reumah. Rizpah. Salome. Sapphira. Sera. Sheerah. Shelomit. Shiprah. Shua. Syntyche. Tamar I. Tamar II. Tamar III. Taphath. Tharbis. Timnah. Tirzah. Zeresh. Zeruiah. Zibiah. Zillah. Zilpah. Zuleika.

Acknowledgement to Country

I would like to acknowledge the Aboriginal and Torress Strait Islanders as the traditional custodians of the land.

I also extend my recognition to the Jagera and the Meanjin peoples to whose lands, I wrote this book on.

Finally, I pay my respects to the Jagera and Turrbal Elders past, present and emerging.

Abigail
(1 Samuel 25)

Shalom!
My name is Abigail.
I was a humble woman who was married in
spite:
To a wealthy scoundrel named Nabal the
Carmelite.

Combining my wealth and wisdom, I appeared
before King David.
After I did, King David had my plea accepted.

Indeed, King David did not war against my
husband or his household too.
Making me feel safe all through.

Later, when my husband died
King David married me.
Making me his third wife
Who gave him a second son (Chileab).

Abigail

Anna the Prophetess
(Luke 2:36-38)

Thank you, God!
My name is Anna.
Being the daughter of Phanuel, I came from the
tribe of Asher.

When I was married, I lived with my husband
For seven years,
Before my husband died, making me a widow
For seventy-seven years.
As a widow, I mourned for a bit
But, didn't depart from the temple
I worshipped God as deemed fit.

When I was of age, eighty-four to be exact
I witnessed Jesus-God- incarnate: fact.
With thanksgiving, I came to greet the child
As, well as his mother Mary and father Joseph.
Indeed, I understood what the arrival of Jesus
meant.
Redemption for the people of Jerusalem.

Anna the Prophetess

Bathsheba
(2 Samuel 11; 2 Samuel 12; 1 Kings 1; 1 Kings 2)

Your Highness,
My name is Bathesheba.
Being the daughter of Eliam,
I was quickly married to a soldier named Uriah.

One day, after my daily bathing,
I was summoned, to see King David.
Alas, King David lied with me,
Resulting in a later pregnancy.

In turn, King David summoned my husband:
Uriah.
Attempting to have him return back home to
Cover the fact that I: Basheba;
Would soon become a mother.

Yet, Uriah refused to go back home,
Claiming his loyalty to protect the throne.
So, King David devised another plan.
Resulting in my husband at battle, to be slain.
When I heard the news, I was distraught.
Sure, I didn't love Uriah,
But we never fought.
After Uriah's funeral, King David then married me;
Hoping to support our son equally.

Understandably, the prophet Nathan,
prophesied a curse:
Where King David would lose the infant
conceived in adultery.
Indeed, this happened, according to the
prophecy.

Fortunately, I was ensured that I would have a
second son.
And as this happened, King David and I, named
him Solomon.
Solomon, our beloved son, reigned from 968–
928 BCE.
He was the successor of King David's kingdom
And legacy.

Bathsheba

Candace
(Acts 8:27-39)

Salam.
My name is Candace.
I was the queen of the Ethiopians.
When the apostle Philip met a eunuch of great
authority.
I too, was inspired, and converted to
Christianity.

With all my wealth and power,
I recognized that there was something more to
life.
Truly, my hundreds, if not thousands, of people
Under my sight
Could not satisfy.

Despite the wars I waged,
And the kingdoms I took down.
When I surrendered my heart to Jesus Christ,
My purpose was found.

Candace

Chloe
(1 Corinthians 1:11)

Peace to you!
My name is Chloe.
Being a respected member of the church in
Corinth, I played a vital role in informing.

Mainly, I informed St. Paul on the divisions and
issues on the rise,
That came from the Corinthian congregation;
With no surprise.

As my household was in contact with Paul,
regularly;
Our communication allowed him to address,
And offer guidance for the Corinthians, and
Profess.

Eventually, this guidance led to St Paul's two
letters;
Addressed to the Corinthian church.
These letters served as a reminder: scrutiny,
Of the importance of open communication and
Unity.

My actions for peace, helped bring about
positive change.
Within the Corinthian congregation, again.

Ultimately, my communication and empathy
Strengthened:
Corinthians' relationship with God,
As well as one another.

Chloe

Claudia
(2 Timothy 4:21)

Salvete!
My name is Claudia.
Being the granddaughter of Emperor Augustus,
I was officially a Roman princess.

As Pontius Pilate was my husband, I witnessed;
Several trials including Christ Jesus'.
After having a terrible dream,
I alerted my husband,
That Jesus Christ was the Son of God;
Not just "a prophet".

Alas, Pontius Pilate refused to listen,
So then I took the path of Christian conversion.
Sooner than later, I was with St Paul in Rome,
Devoting my life, to his mission-
leaving my Home.

Being a new Christian woman, I was close to
the faith.
Preaching out Christ's message,
With the apostles, every day.

Claudia

Deborah
(Judges 4; Judges 5)

Order in the Court!
My name is Deborah.
I worked as a judge.
The only female judge to be exact.
Performing at a judicial function,
As a matter of fact.

Being a decisive figure- a Judge, I used to hold
court;
While sitting beneath a palm tree, I could
gather my thoughts.
I helped the people solve their problems.
Famously, I helped Barak, commander of an
army of Israel;
Whom the Lord wanted to fight an enemy
named Sisera.
But, Barak refused to fight Sisera,
Unless accompanied by me- Deborah.
Indeed, I went along, and defeated Sisera's
army.
Moreover, during the battle, when Sisera
escaped to a tent;
I guided Jael to kill Sisera- in his sleep- with no
relent.

Deborah

Dinah
(Genesis 30:21; Genesis 34; Gensis 46:15)

Shalom!
My name is Dinah.
I was the daughter of Jacob and Leah.
When I was grown, I was abducted and raped,
Near the city of Shechem- it was profane.
The son of Hamor the Hivite, raped me,
All because I refused his offer to marry.
In retaliation, Hamor suggested to my father
-Jacob,
For two peoples to initiate a policy.
This policy was based on commercial and social
contact.
And my brothers: Simeon and Levi, pretended
To agree to this contract.
Hence, after the operations, while
The men were still weakened,
Simeon and Levi attacked the city.
By this attack, all the males were killed
instantly,
Including Shechem and Hamor- who abducted
me.
As time passed, I finally found romance;
Thereby, married Job, a truly righteous man.

Dinah

Dorcas
(Acts 9:36-42)

How can I serve you?
My name is Dorcas, but you can call me Tabitha!
I was a disciple of Jesus by following his
teachings.
My service was to look after the poor, widows,
and make clothing.

As I always did good, helping those in need;
When I suddenly got sick and died, it brought
misery.
Consequently, two men were sent to urge Peter
The apostle, to come to Joppa;
And as he came, I was already placed upstairs,
In preparation for burial.

My friends and the widows say they were mourning.
Until St Peter arrived, they had no comforting.
After they showed Peter the clothes I had made for them.
He sent them all out of the room; Got on his knees and prayed.
After he prayed, he said : *"Tabitha, get up!"*,
I opened my eyes and sat up.
St Peter then called for all my friends to come back,
Presented me- a living Tabitha- at last.
My coming back to life became known all over Joppa,
And, as a result, many more people believed in the Lord.

Hopefully, my story including my initial departure,
Inspires you to have an impact, use your gifts,
Taking care of those around you,
And those who are further.

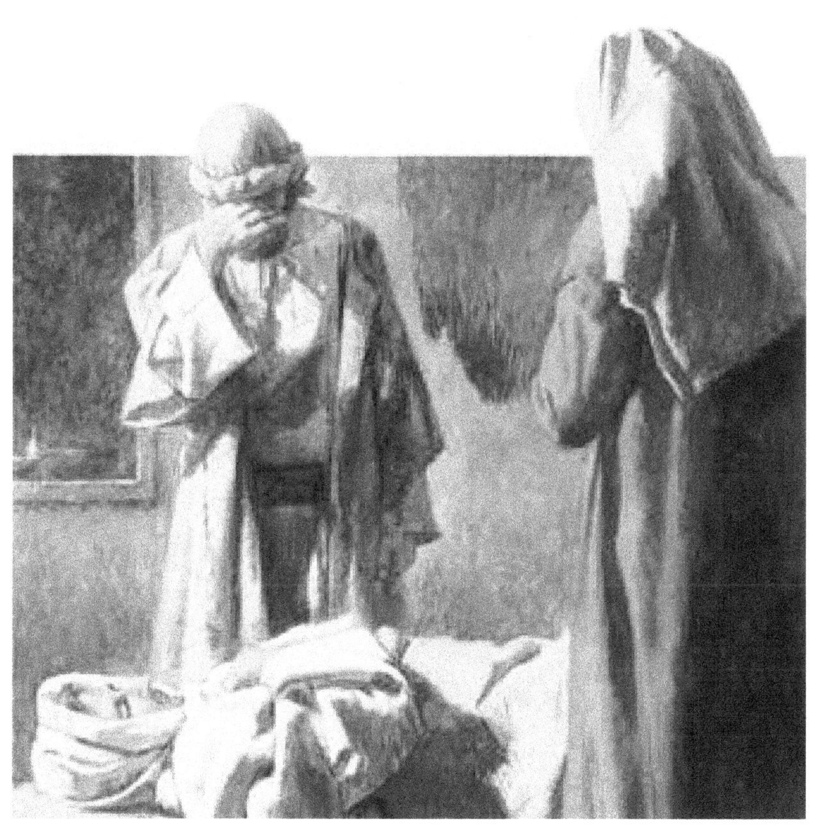

Dorcas

Elizabeth
(Luke 1: 5-80)

God is with you!
My name is Elizabeth,
And I am a descendant of Aaron's family.
I married Zechariah, also a descendant of
Aaron.
As such, Zechariah was a serving priest for the
masses.

As I had learned the lessons, I lived a life;
Of piety as a priest's daughter, and as a priest's
wife.
Hence, being a righteous woman but childless,
Zechariah and I, were seen by others as
unfortunate,
But God saw us as faithful and upright.

Undoubtedly, it had been my dream and desire
to become a mother,
Just as Zechariah yearned to also be a father.

Despite praying for a child,
Zechariah and I became old,
Before accepting that this parenting dream of
ours,
Would, unlikely, be realized.

Nevertheless, in line with my name meaning
"God is my oath"
I lived my life with love, service, and hope.

Then, on the miraculous day where Zechariah;
Had been chosen to go to the temple,
He burned incense before the Lord,
Before the apparition of Archangel Gabriel.

The Archangel Gabriel announced a message
From God the Most High;
Confirming that Zechariah and I, would finally
have a child.

Breaking tradition, Archangel Gabriel stated:
How our child's name would be John, not
Zechariah as stated.
He also confirmed how John would grow up to
be.
The Messiah's forerunner, a sincere ministry.
Alas, as Zechariah asked the Archangel Gabriel
On how this could happen on earth;
Zechariah became speechless,
And remained speechless, until after John's
birth.

As Zechariah's time of service ended,
He came to me when I conceived,
Then I stated with no tremble:
"The Lord has done this for me.

In these days he has shown His favour,
And taken away my disgrace among the people".

Six months later, the Archangel Gabriel visited
my relative St Mary,
There, he told her what was going to happen in
Her life, and on what happened to me.

After St Mary's encounter with Archangel
Gabriel,
She went to visit me, swiftly.

St Mary stayed with me for three consecutive
months.
Before returning back home
To give birth to her Son.

Now as King Herod had issued a decree to kill
newborn boys in Israel,
My dear husband Zechariah, tried to hide John
at the temple's altar-inside.
However, this didn't stop the soldiers from
killing Zechariah, with pride.
Thankfully, John was safely missed,
And the angels of the Lord carried our son:
Raising him in the wilderness.

Elizabeth

Elisheba
(Exodus 6:23)

Shalom alekhem!
My name is Elisheba,
The daughter of Amminadav,
Sister of Nahson,
And most renowned as the wife of high priest:
Aaron.

Aaron and I had a total of four sons.
Starting with Nadab, Abihu,
To Eleazar, and finally Ithamar.

Despite never appearing in any story,
I brought awareness to Moses and Aaron's
Genealogy.
In other words, my inclusion contributed to the
Prominence of the lineage;
Indicating how women- like me- were vital to
Their children's destinies.

Elisheba

Queen Esther
(Esther 1- Esther 10)

Shalom, my beloved people!
My name is Hadassah.
I was the daughter of Avichayil, son of Kish;
A descendant of King Saul,
Whose father also bore the name Kish.

Ever since both my parents died, when I was a
child, My cousin Mordecai took me to his home-
to reside.

Now, as I had no interest in becoming queen,
I just submitted to fate making me chosen.
I even allowed for my name to be changed:
From Hadassah to Esther- a Persian name.

Being now married to the Persian King:
Artaxerxes,
Mordechai advised me to keep my Judaism faith
a secret.
Moreover, to maintain my Jewish life
undercover,
I had a total of seven maids that -for me-looked
after.

Each maid served me on a different weekday.
Thus, only the Shabbat maid would not notice
how I prayed.

Under the influence of my husband's advisor:
Haman,
Artaxerxes decreed that all Jews in his
expansive empire,
Would be- in a single day- slaughtered!.

Such a decree, placed myself in grave jeopardy,
As well as my people who I cared for deeply.
Hence, after my maids and I fasted and prayed:
To God, for three days.
I then petitioned to the King, right away.

Consequently, my petition helped reverse the
legislation.
Leaving the wicked advisor- Haman-to be
killed.
Indeed, my act of courage, helped save and
defend;
The Jewish nation, during King Artaxerxes'
reign.

Queen Esther

Eunice
(2 Timothy 1:5; 2 Timothy 1: 14-15)

Yia sas!
My name is Eunice.
I was seen as a model Christian mother:
faithful, wise, and diligent.
Although I married an unbeliever, I raised my
Son, Timothy,
To follow God's ways, from the earliest
moment.

Raising Timothy was not easy in the city of
Lystra;
Especially as the city was an immoral kind of
one.
People worshiped foreign gods,
Except for me- Eunice and my mother, Lois.

By being steadfast in our beliefs,
We raised Timothy to know the Torah,
Although uncircumcised.
And to live an obedient, God-fearing life.

As Timothy's father – my husband- died early
on,
St Paul took Timothy under his wing;
For service, ministry and to disciple him.

Even in St Paul's final days,
He mustered all his strength and passion,
To address one of his young disciples- my
Timothy,
Whom he had come to love as a son, Right away.

Also, from the dank Roman prison cell,
St Paul penned a letter to encourage;
Young Timothy, my son.
Reminding him to practice, guard, and preach
to everyone.

Moreover, this letter opened up to say:
Paul's gratitude for myself- Eunice,
And my mother-Lois, just the same.
For we were the ladies responsible for laying
the groundwork;
Particularly for Paul's protégé- Timothy-
And his faith with great work.

Eunice

Euodia
(Philippians 4:2–3; Ephesians 4:31; John 13:34–35)

Zdravo!
My name is Euodia.
Although I am mentioned in only one short
Bible passage;
I played a role, in spreading St Paul's message.

As I directly contended at Paul's side,
in the cause of spreading the Gospel to the city
of Philippi,
I worked with Syntyche, and had begun a
Women's prayer meeting.

However, I must note that at times, Syntyche,
and I,
had some disagreements over things.
But we worked above;
Preserving the original purpose of the early
church: unconditional love.

Euodia

Eve
(Genesis 2; Genesis 3)

Apple of my eye!
My name is Eve.
In Hebrew this meant 'help'.
Rightly so, as I helped Adam,
While being the first woman on earth.

Being the first woman, I was also the first wife;
I was also dubbed as
The "Mother of All the Living."

Even though my accomplishments were many.
Little is known, apart from me eating fruit.
The forbidden tree.

Indeed, the serpent was so devious and sly,
I couldn't tell what was wrong or right.
So, I believed the serpent, instead of always
trusting in God.
And as a result, Adam, and I, were banished at
once.

While leaving the Garden of Eden, I wept with
shame and dismay.
Yet, I had hope that God would unite us-
Humanity, again, one day.

Eve

Gomer (Hosea 1:3; Hosea 3:2)

Salaam.
My name is Gomer. To put it simply, my name
meant 'fulfilment'.
Which was fitting for God and Israel's covenant.

I had no intention to marry or settle down.
It wasn't until God commanded Hosea to marry
me in town.

Being the daughter of Diblaim, I should have
been taught proper conduct,
Especially as Hosea was the one to prophesy to
Israel.
Sadly, I was a harlot, just like my mother;
Making my mother and I, the topic of gossip
and slander.

After two sons and a daughter with Hosea,
Hosea was emotionally attached, and felt
obligated to me.

Even when God tested him to leave me,
Hosea passed the test, learning that a husband
And wife relationship is not easy.

Before I knew it, I also learned that my
Marriage was an allegory,
Of God's everlasting covenant with the nation
of Israel,
Even when Israel was unfaithful.

Gomer

Hannah the Prophetess
(1 Samuel)

I am grateful to meet you!
My name is Hannah; Meaning to have 'grace or
favour'.
Being a prophetess and worshipper at
Jerusalem;
I struggled with infertility,
Which made me a spectacle, by women.

As an infertile woman, I struggled to find
self-worth.
Despite my husband's- Elkanah- efforts to help,
I was determined to keep asking God for
children.
And through faith in God, I became a mother of
six children;
Including Samuel the prophet.

To detail further on my first son- Samuel,
I vowed to God, that he would be in the temple.
Thus, after giving my first son to God above,
I was blessed to have five more children to love.

Eli the priest brought up Samuel in the temple,
Assuring me that Samuel would be brought up
well;
And serve as God's faithful prophet.

Hannah

Jehosheba
(2 Chronicles)

Hello, nice to meet you.
My name is Jehosheba.
I was the princess of Judah in the 9th century
B.C. With a lineage of royalty.

My grandfather was the righteous King
Jehoshaphat; Then, my father was King
Jehoram;
Followed by my brother- Ahaziah, who was also
King of the land.

When I swooped up Joash- my nephew, just a
child but destined to be king,
Hence, I brought him to the temple, with my
next of kin.

Indeed, I nursed Joash in secret for some time,
Until God revealed it was safe for us not to hide.

Being the seventh year for the right time to
come,
Jehoiada [the priest, my husband] sent for
captains;
All of which summed up to being over
hundreds.

In addition, Jehoiada, brought guards on swiftly,
Helping us, enter the Lord's house, quickly.

Jehosheba

Jemima
(Job 42:14)

Pleased to meet you!
My name is Jemimah;
It's a Hebrew name meaning "dove".
Rightly so, as I lived in peace, freedom, and
love.

Being the oldest, of Job's total three daughters,
Which God had planned,
I was known as one of the loveliest women,
In all of the land.

Jemima

Joanna
(Luke 8:1-3; Luke 23: 55-56; Luke 24:10)

Shalom Aleichem!
My name is Joanna.
A name that means "God's gift";
Which is ironic because I was not an initial
Follower of God.

In fact, I was one of several women in the Bible,
Who, was healed of "evil spirits and diseases"
inside.
After Jesus Christ had healed me, I chose to join
Him
As well as the twelve disciples, in the ministry.

After my conversion to Christianity,
I used my means and influence.
All of which came from my husband Chuza;
For as Chuza was the manager of Herod
Antipas,
He also managed Herod Antipas' household
estate.

Now, being in first-century Judaism, my
conduct was considered scandalous.
As I was a married woman, it was not fit to be
serving with a man.
Yet, my life served as an example of how the
Gospel acts;
Demolishing class barriers and
Social Prejudicial tacts.

Along with Mary Magdalene, Susanna, and
others,
I helped provide food and supplies,
I was also present with Jesus,
On His final journey from Galilee to Jerusalem.

Finally, I was present at Jesus' crucifixion and
burial.
After, women and I returned to the tomb.
We prepared spices and burial ointments,
To anoint Jesus' body with.
And upon discovering the empty tomb,
We ran to report – to the apostles- the news
That just happened.

Joanna

Jochebed
(Exodus 2:1-10)

Shalom Aleichem!
My name is Jochebed;
A name meaning "God's glory", and rightly so!
For God's glory was apparent in my life,
All through.

I was a wise woman, righteous and God-fearing.
By merit of my good deeds, I gave birth three
leaders.
They were the leaders of the Exodus
generation:
Moses, Aaron, and Miriam.

When Moses was born, I saw how beautiful he
was. So,
I sought to save him from Pharaoh's death
decree.

Thus, I prepared the 'ark' for Moses;
It was a basket made of bulrushes:
Material capable of withstanding contact.
Next, I placed Moses- while in the basket- in the
Nile River.

Praying that someone would find him alive.
Thankfully be to God, Pharaoh's daughter found
him.
Pharaoh's daughter then allowed me to nurse
Moses for three months.
Right after this time, I was forced to obey the
Decree of Pharaoh, at once.

As any mother can imagine, giving up your
child is heartbreakingly sad;
But, I held onto God's promise,
And submitted to His plan.

Jochebed

Judith
(Judith 1- Judith 16)

Shalom alekhem!
My name is Judith;
A name which means "to be praised".
Who would have thought,
That I would live up to my name?

A long time ago, a powerful general:
Holofernes, Declared war against Bethulia.
With a great army,
My people were certain to have a loss.

Holofernes besieged the city for many days,
Making sure no food or drink could come our
way.
While the Israelites suffered tremendously
during this siege,
I was determined to not fall, in the verge of
surrendering.

Since my husband died unexpectedly,
I had been a widow in mourning for three
years,

Hence, I was courageous to devise a plan,
Where my people would be free in the land.

First, I rebuked the leaders of Bethulia for their
intention to surrender,
And declared that God would act through my
endeavour.
Second, I removed my mourning attire And
Dressed in beautiful clothes and jewels,
Before preparing a bag of wine and kosher
cheese.

Third, I waited until nightfall,
And was accompanied only by my maid,
To exit the besieged city,
Under cover of darkness in the way.

As I walked into the enemy camp,
I eventually entered the royal pavilion.
Lo and behold, there was Holofernes looking in.

Since I as exceedingly beautiful,
Holofernes could not resist.
And I found favour in his eyes.
So much so, that he invited me to come with.

In deceit, I gave him compliments on his
Wisdom and skill;
I even commented that Israel has sinned,
And that he should deal with what he wills.
After gaining his trust, he agreed to invite me
into his tent.
Inside the tent, I feasted with him, hiding my
contempt.

After Holofernes drank a great deal of wine, he
fell asleep;
I took his sword from his bedpost where it
hung,
Then I cut his head off, in one clean sweep.

Taking Holofernes' head and placing it in my
bag,
My maidservant passed unnoticed through the
camp.

Until I reached the gates of Bethulia;
I summoned the gatekeepers,
Instructing them to place the general's head,
So that the army would see it, after they slept.

Unquestionably, when the general's men found
his body in the morning.
As well as his head positioned on the gate- high,
The men fled quickly,
Confirming the war was over;
And that my people, dominated this time.

Judith

Julia
(Romans 16:15)

Salve!
My name is Julia.
Married to Philologus, I was a Christian woman
At Rome,
Whom St Paul sent his salutations to.

My husband and I, joined Nereus and Olympas,
Offering our lives as holy and pleasing to God.
I understood that Christians are saints,
Not based on anything done,
But all because of standing in Jesus the Christ.
Such a standing follows His perfect example:
An example of love and righteousness inside.

Julia

Kerren-Happuch
(Job 42:14)

Lovely to meet you!
My name is Keren-Happuch;
It's a Hebrew name meaning "horn of
antimony".
Rightly so, as I lived in calm harmony.

Being the third of Job's total three daughters,
Which God had planned,
I was known as one of the loveliest women,
In all of the land.

Kerren-Happuch

Keziah
(Job 42:14)

Pleasant to meet you!
My name is Keziah;
It's a Hebrew name meaning "sweet scented
spice".
Rightly so, as I was compassionate and nice.

Being the second of Job's total three daughters,
Which God had planned,
I was known as one of the loveliest women,
In all of the land.

Keziah

Leah
(Genesis 29:17)

Shalom alekhem!
My name is Leah.
I was the elder daughter of Laban.
When my father tricked Jacob to marry me.
It was apparent that Jacob, had no feelings for
me.

My sister Rachel, whose names meant "cow"
and "ewe".
Was loved by Jacob and he married her too.
He loved her so much even though she was
barren,
In return, God gave me many sons,
As a consolation.

Through my sons Levi and Judah in particular,
I was the matriarch of both the priestly
(Levite),
And the royal (Judahite) tribes in Israel.

Leah

Lois
(2 Timothy 1:5)

Shalom alekhem!
My name is Lois;
A name meaning "superior and beautiful".

Being the maternal grandmother of Timothy,
It brought me gladness to see St Paul take him
under his wing.
Timothy, to whom Paul wrote his final and most
intimate epistle,
Turned out to be a vital part of the ministry.

With my daughter- Eunice, we followed Christ,
While supporting Timothy after St Paul's
martyrdom;
To always do what is right.

Lois

Lydia of Thyataria
(Acts 16)

My door is always open!
My name is Lydia of Thyataria.
As my name suggests, I lived in the city of
Thyatira;
A city located in Asia Minor, at best.

My city was known for its purple dye and
textiles.
Hence, being a woman of status and wealth,
I sold cloth to wealthy clients in Philippi, as
well.

Also, as I was the first Christian convert, in the
colonial Roman city of Philippi,
I was courageous and confident,
To be involved in the ministry.

Thus, in place of selling wealthy items- my
former life;
I acted as a benefactress of the Christian
church,
Day and night.

Lydia of Thyataria

Mary and Martha
(Luke 10)

Marhaba!
Our names are Mary and Martha;
We're sisters with Lazarus- one brother.

Living in Bethany- two miles from Jerusalem,
Our family was well known to many men.
We were even more known, when Jesus raised
Lazarus;
Especially as Lazarus had been dead for three
days, in a tomb.

I-Martha, prioritised completing tasks.
Indeed, as I was a practical, impulsive, and
short-tempered lady,
I even scolded Jesus, to get Mary to help me.

In response to my scolding, Jesus taught me to
reflect;
And consider being more present and calm.

Enter in me- Mary- I was like the Apostle John:
A person who was reflective, loving, and calm.
Even still, Martha was a remarkable woman
and sister;
For it was quite rare -in our day- for a woman
to manage her own affairs.
Hopefully, you can learn from us- Martha and
Mary,
Thereby balance your Christian walk to have
both qualities.
What we mean is that at times you will be
inclined,
To let your service be hindered by your busy
lives;
But on the upside, you will find time free from
distractions,
To spend more time with Jesus and applying
His word through actions.

Mary and Martha

St Mary the Theotokos
(Luke 1:39; Luke 2:1)

Behold the Maidservant of the Lord!
My name is St Mary.
Many call me St Mary the "Theotokos"
Confirming that I was the mother of God.

Flashback to my early years,
From my birth to when I was 12 years old,
I stayed at the Temple.
There, I would clean, pray, and serve.

When I turned 12 years old, I was 'of age'
And had to leave the temple,
To live in the society of Nazareth instead.

Before I knew it, I was betrothed to Joseph
there;
But that didn't stop me from serving and
committing to prayer.
After Archangel Gabriel appeared to me,
It was clear that I was to fulfil the Messiah
prophecy.

The Messiah prophecy entailed that a virgin,
Would give birth the Son.
Hence, Archangel confirmed that the Virgin was
me,
And that I couldn't tell just anyone.

The only people that knew at the time,
Were my husband- Joseph- and one relative,
Named Elizabeth, who was understanding and
kind.

After the birth of the Son- Jesus Christ- in a
humble manger,
Joseph and I fled for safety to the land of Egypt-
free of danger.
Indeed, we stayed in Egypt for two whole years,
And after being informed -by the angel- to
return back.
We returned to Nazareth, with no turning back.

Bringing up Jesus with Joseph, was a special
task.
Jesus was not like a son that anyone had.
His humanity and divinity never parted away,
Not even for a twinkle of eye, or in His time of
play.

From the birth of Jesus and the presentation of
him in the Temple,
Jesus' was not just a pure child, or so simple.
I still recall when the Magi came,
Gifting Jesus gold, frankincense and myrrh to
sustain.

I also remember when Jesus was 12 years old,
And Joseph and I lost Him in the Passover at
Jerusalem.
This made Joseph and I worry and feel
ashamed.
But Jesus reassured us that His purpose is big,
so we can't stand in His way.

Even the marriage at Cana in Galilee,
Although my name is not used.
Confirmed my attempt to see Jesus making,
A miracle- turning water to wine- without
hesitating.

Over all the years, He was teaching and
involved in the ministry;
I never prepared myself enough, to see Him be
crucified on the cross,
For the whole world and me.

Indeed, while I was stationed at His cross, I
remember my heart burning in pain, So my
Beloved Son, and Saviour, entrusted me, To live
with His disciple John, from that very day.

St Mary the Theotokos

Mary Magdalene
(Luke 8:1-2; Luke 23:55; Luke 24:10; Mark 15:40; Mark 16:7)

Shalom aleichem!
My name is Mary Magdalene.
I was a Jewish woman from the fishing town
Magdala:
A town on the western shore of the Sea of
Galilee.

My name is mentioned twelve times in the
Gospels,
More than most of the apostles.
As Mark and Luke recorded, Jesus healed me
From seven demons.

Being one of the many Marys that followed
Jesus,
I never forgot how my life changed with Jesus
healing my ailment.
Internal gratitude fuelled my generosity and
dedication.

I also remained until Jesus' body was taken
down from the cross.
Following to witness Joseph of Arimathea's
burial of Jesus.
Since I knew the exact location where Jesus had
been laid to rest.
I knew the path so well, that I could trace my
steps.

So days later, I went to the location and found,
That Jesus' body was not around.
After crying for what seemed like a year,
I heard a man- who turned out to be Jesus-
calling me to hear.

As Jesus explained He rose from the dead;
As He had previously said,
I ran to tell the apostles all that Jesus had said.

Mary Magdalene

Michal
(1 Samuel 19: 11-17; 2 Samuel 3:5; 2 Samuel 6:23; 2 Samuel 12:8)

Hi there love,
My name is Michal.
I was the daughter of the infamous King- Saul,
And married his archnemesis- David.

In love with David, I proved my loyalty to him.
Particularly when I saved David from my
father's attack- on the whim.
Evidently, I was praised for my loyalty to David,
And my rejection of my father's authority to kill
him.
However, when I later disrespected David
publicly,
I was punished with a terrible prophecy.

The prophecy entailed that I, to my dying day,
Would bear no children, not a single day.
Nevertheless, God had mercy on me, the day I
died,
And I gave birth to a son, before forever closing
my eyes.

Michal

Miriam
(Exodus 2: 1-10; Numbers 12:1-6)

God has delivered us!
My name is Miriam.

I'm best known for helping to deliver Moses at
the Nile River- with ease.
Also, for leading the Hebrew women in singing,
Dancing, and playing drums,
After crossing the Red Sea.

Later, my brother Aaron and I challenge the
actions and authority of Moses.
I understood leadership to embrace diverse
voices, female and male.
Sadly, due to speaking out, God punished me
with a disease.
Fortunately, after seven days, I was healed.

However, after my punishment, I never spoke
again,
Nor, was I spoken to by women or men.
Indeed, I disappeared altogether from the
narrative,
Until the announcement of my death and burial
at Kadesh.

Nevertheless, centuries later, prophecy still
remembers me;
As the inaugurator of Israel's drums, dances,
and song.
An equal of Moses and Aaron's ministry- all
along.

Miriam

Naomi
(Ruth 1-Ruth 4)

Call me Mara!
But my name is Naomi;
A name meaning "sweetness".
However, my life was not all that, you will get
what I mean.

My married life opened up with a great famine,
Sending my Judean family across the Jordan,
And all the way to Moab, a foreign land.

My husband Elimelech, and our children,
Were not prepared for God's derision.
After Elimelech's death, Naomi relied on her
two sons;
Both of whom married Moabite wives.

Alas, both of my sons died suddenly,
I became a widow and childless woman,
instantly.
Orpah and Ruth- my daughter in laws,
Were inclined to not leave me alone.

With my persuasion, I convinced Orpah to
leave,
Only Ruth insisted that she would stay with me.
Then, upon hearing that the Lord had
Restored food to Judah,
Ruth and I began the journey home.

When the women of the Judah town, noticed
me,
I instructed them not to call me "Naomi"
But "Mara" (meaning "bitter") instead.

Fortunately, my story did not end there,
But I will leave it to Ruth to detail what
happened,
A miracle involving a man called Boaz,
Who graciously married her.

Naomi

Orpah
(Ruth 1:1-9)

I've gotta go my own way. My name is Orpah,
And I'm well-known for, Taking Naomi's offer to
return back to my home.

Being a widow, I knew that life would be hard,
But I am glad that at least, I had a choice,
Although not easy.

With Ruth staying with Naomi,
I could mourn in solace and peace,
The ten years with my husband, filled my
memories.

Orpah

Phoebe
(Romans 16:1–2)

How can I serve you?
My name is Phoebe.
I lived in Cenchreae,
A coastal town,
About five miles southeast,
Of the city of Corinth.

St Paul introduced me,
As a woman of high standing
At the Cenchrae church,
Setting the stage for me, to have a successful
pivot.

He asked Roman believers to aid me- a
deaconess- in my visit,
Making me a part of a larger cohort of serving
women.

Women named Chloe, Nympha, Apphia, Euodia,
As well as Syntyche and Junia,
Whom were stationed to serve with me,
Expanding the Gospel and St Paul's ministry.

Phoebe

Priscilla
(Acts 18:1-3; Acts 18:21; Romans 16: 3-4; 1 Corinthians 16:19)

Yia sas!
My name is Priscilla; A Hebrew name meaning
"old" and "venerable".
But I was far from just that,
I was lively, generous, and compassionate.

My husband Aquila, a name meaning "an eagle",
Was a tentmaker like me,
We both had an eye for detail and accuracy.
With a sharp eye to make tents, Aquila also
could guard;
Against enemies that tried to prevent,
The message of God.

Overall, Aquila and I had the gift of being able
to make tents.
Along with using our tents' funds to further the
mission.

We even opened our homes,
So people could enter and learn about God.
This gift of hospitality offered to guests,
Fulfilled their wishes to gain knowledge about
God.

Priscilla

Rachel
(Genesis 29; Genesis 35:24; Genesis 46:15–18)

Shalom Aleichem!
My name is Rachel.
I lived in Mesopotamia for all my life.
And when Jacob met me at a well.
He announces our kinship and asked me to be
his wife.

My father- Laban- made Jacob work to make
me his wife.
In fact, Jacob worked a total of 14 years -what a
life.

When I was married, I spent a lot of my time
trying to conceive,
Eventually God had mercy on me.
And so, I bored two sons- Joseph and Benjamin.

However, at Benjamin's birth, I died at
childbirth.
Leaving a legacy of my two sons,
Both, who became two of the twelve tribes, of
Israel.

Rachel

Rahab
(Joshua 2)

Salam,
My name is Rahab.
I lived in the city of Jericho,
A city located near the Jordan River.

Before the Israelites cross the Jordan,
Joshua sent men to scout out the land.
Arriving in Jericho, Joshua and Salmon decided
to spend the night,
At my house- a former prostitute- in town.

When Jericho's ruler tried to apprehend them,
I made sure to successfully hide them.
Due to hiding them so well, I helped them
escape;
Through the window, thus saving their lives,
that were on stake.

In return, my extended family and I, were
spared.
Hence, when the destruction of Jericho
occurred,
We became part of the people Israel,
Safe, comfortable, with our lives spared.

Even my nucleur family:
Salmon, my husband and Boaz, our son,
Became part of the Christ's lineage,
A lineage of the chosen Israel.

Rahab

Rebekah
(Genesis 24:60; Genesis 25:19-28;
Genesis 27: 5-6, Genesis 27:11;
Genesis 27:15; Genesis 27: 42)

Shalom Aleichem!
My name is Rebekah.
I was born at the same time that Isaac,
Who was then twenty-six years old, was bound
On the altar.

When bound there, God revealed to Abraham-
At Mount Moriah,
Sending an angel to command Abraham to not
Sacrifice his only son.
God then also disclosed to him,
By the spirit of divine inspiration,
That Isaac's bride- me- had already been born.

Abraham thought that his only son and heir
was about to die,
But God had brought me into the world- Isaac's
future wife.

Although my family and those among, lived
deceitful,
I – by God's grace- was not adversely
influenced,
But grew up as "a lily among thorns."

I was the recipient of special blessings:
The well water rose up to me, the dough I
kneaded was blessed,
And the cloud was visible over only my tent.

God revealed His plan to me,
When both of Isaac and I's sons, were still in my
womb.
And, with her prophetic perception,
I knew that Esau would one day plan to kill his
brother- Jacob.

Sure, it broke my heart that the brothers could
not be together.
Getting along and going strong.
But I had to use my ability to distinguish,
Between righteous Jacob and the wicked Esau.
Hence, I aided in the execution of God's plan,
By causing Jacob to receive Isaac's blessing,
Instead of Esau, as planned.

Rebekah

Rhoda
(Acts 12:12–15)

Welcome home!
My name is Rhoda;
And I'm briefly mentioned once in the Bible.

I was a servant girl in the house of Mary,
Who was the mother of John Mark.

When a group of people had gathered at Mary's
house to pray for St Peter,
Who had been arrested and put in prison by
Herod. Our prayers were answered;
And God sent an angel to free St Peter from
prison.

After freeing St Peter from prison, the angel
left,
Thus, St Peter travelled to Mary's house
instead.

Hence, when Peter knocked on the door,
I was sent to answer it.
Upon recognizing St Peter's voice,
I was so excited that I could not open the door
as planned.

Rather, I ran back to the group of praying
people,
Declaring to them, that the person at the door,
was St Peter.

The praying people told me, I was mad.
But St Peter kept knocking with command.

Finally, the group of people, opened the door.
All were surprised to find that I had been right.
And from that day, I remained more than a
servant girl,
But a woman, faithful and trusting in God,
All day and all night.

Rhoda

Ruth
(Ruth 1- Ruth 4)

Shalom Aleichem!
My name is Ruth.
I had a rocky start to marriage,
Losing my beloved husband after ten years,
with no damage.

Sticking by my mother-in-law- Naomi,
Despite being a Moabite immigrant from birth,
I remained hopeful that Judah would see my
worth.

At first, it was hard to adjust in Judah,
But I didn't stop.
Expressing my deference to Naomi, I worked;
And not long after,
Boaz saw me gleaning the crops.

For my devotion and loyalty to my mother-in
-law , Boaz allowed me to glean in his field, And
further arranged modes for my safety.

I responded with appropriate deference,
Appreciating his favour to my foreignness.
Clearly, Boaz recognized my distinctiveness;
And called for people to witness,
Before he took me for marriage.

Ruth

The Samaritan Woman (St Photini) (John 4:5-30)

Would you like a drink of water?
My former name is the Samaritan Woman,
Afterwards, I changed my life,
So, St Photini, became my new name outside.

Starting when I went by the "Samaritan woman",
I remember going to the well everyday.
I would go during the middle of the day.
Yet despite my efforts to see no one,
I met Jesus Christ one day.

Initially, I was thankful He wasn't a man from my past.
However, He was a Jewish man, asking for water from my flask.
Being already vulnerable because of my wrongdoings,
I thought it was some kind of warning.
Yet, when Jesus talked with wisdom and love,
I immediately recognized He was from God, above.

With His acceptance, I was comfortable enough
to hear Him out.
In turn, sharing my own self-doubt.
Then He invited me to get in touch;
Particularly, with the thirst in my soul, at once.

I then, finally, realized I had found someone,
Who could fulfill my deepest longings, unlike
anyone.

So, from that moment forward, I ran to Samaria.
Spreading the Good news.
The people were enlightened but also confused.

No matter the chatter, I chose to leave behind;
All the hurt and past shortcomings,
To become Saint Photini.
A manifestation of my new life.

The Samaritan Woman (St Photini)

Sarah, wife of Abraham
(Genesis 17:15–21)

Shalom Aleichem!
My name is originally Sarai,
Before God changed it to Sarah, instead.

My role as Abraham's wife,
Was to foreshadow Israel's later bondage,
And ultimate release.
Initially, I was unable to have children for most
Of my life.
I doubted God's promise of having a son, many
times.
Hence, I eventually used Hagar as a surrogate
to birth Ishmael.
Such an impulsive decision made me feel
unwell.
Finally, at ninety years of age, God blessed me
With the birth of Isaac.
After securing Isaac's position in the family as
Abraham's heir,
I disappeared from Genesis,
But remain remembered,
As the people's ancestress.

Sarah, wife of Abraham

Sarah, wife of Tobias
(Tobit 3:8-17):

Shalom Aleichem!
My name is Sarah,
The one who had seven husbands, Each of
whom died on their wedding night.

As a result, I was initially despairing,
Thinking that no one could dare to marry me,
Especially since I had the demon Asmodeus
interfering.

I remember praying for my death.
God heard my prayer and Tobit's too;
But God didn't answer the way we expected.
Instead, he sent Archangel Raphael to heal both
myself and Tobit.

Fortunately, as Tobit remembered that he had
left,
A large sum of money in Media.
He then sent his son Tobiah to get it.
Tobiah met Archangel Raphael, disguised as a
man,
And they travelled together to Media- a far
land.

On the way, Tobiah was attacked by a large fish,
So Archangel Raphael told him to grab it, kill it,
And remove its gall, heart and liver.

Arriving in Media, Tobiah and Archangel
Raphael,
Stayed at the home of Raguel, my father.
At Archangel Raphael's urging, Tobiah married
me;
And during our wedding night,
Tobiah used the fish's heart and liver,
To drive out Asmodeus with might.

After a wedding feast, Tobiah recovered Tobit's
money.
Next, Tobiah, Archangel Raphael, and I, made
the return trip.
On our arrival, Tobiah rubbed the fish's gall into
Tobit's eyes.
Curing his blindness in time.

Archangel Raphael then revealed his identity.
Before returning to heaven, for eternity.

Sarah, wife of Tobias

Susanna
(Daniel 13)

Shalom Aleichem!
My name is Susanna;
A wealthy Babylonian Jewish woman,
Married to a wealthy man.

Joakim, my husband, took me to live in the
Babylonian diaspora.
All was bliss and well ,
Until two elderly men, wanted to sin with me.

Being the wife of Joakim and daughter of
Hilkiah,
People could not fathom the accusation;
Of me sinning with the elderly men, frivolously.

Thankfully, Daniel the prophet, came to my
defence.
Testing the two wicked and elderly men.
As a result, the two men were charged with
death for the false accusation.
And I was spared from my damning sentence of
death.

At the close of my tale of twists and turns,
My parents and husband rejoice,
Not just because I could live,
But, because I was found pure and innocent.

Susanna

Tryphena and Tryphosa
(Romans 16:12)

Yia sas!
Our names are Tryphena and Tryphosa,
Meaning "luxurious and delicate" inside.
Rightly so, we both were lively sisters,
Living our best lives.

We, along with Persis, had something far more
important in common.
We all loved and served the Lord.

Being devoted followers, we showed our love,
Through devotion by working hard to lay up
eternal treasures in Heaven,
Instead of temporary treasures on earth.

All in all, St Paul was grateful for our work in
the Lord. He showed His gratefulness, by giving
us a shout-out in his letter, as well.

Tryphena and Tryphosa

Zipporah
(Exodus 2:21-22; Exodus 4:20;
Exodus 18: 3-4)

Halo!
My name is Zipporah,
I was a Midianite woman,
Whom later became the wife of Moses.

I met Moses after he fled from pharaoh,
To settle among my people -the Midianites.
My people were an Arab people who had the
desert areas,
Located in southern Transjordan,
Northern Arabia, occupied.

Next, when Moses saw me and my six sisters,
Daughters of Reuel- priest of Midian;
He rescued us from the shepherds,
Who were harassing us to fill their water jugs.

In gratitude, Reuel offered Moses hospitality,
Then gave me- his daughter- in marriage,
Beautifully.

Moses and I had two sons,
The first was named Gershom,
And the second: Eliezer.

My marriage with Moses was one of patience
and love.
I would always stand up for him,
When the Israelites complained he spent too
much time;
Speaking face to face with God.

Zipporah